MONSTERS

Banshees

By Kelli M. Brucken

KIDHAVEN PRESS

An imprint of Thomson Gale, a part of The Thomson Corporation

THOMSON

™

GALE

Detroit • New York • San Francisco • San Diego
New Haven, Conn. • Waterville, Maine • London • Munich

3 9082 10617 5402

For more information, contact
KidHaven Press
27500 Drake Rd.
Farmington Hills, MI 48331-3535
Or you can visit our Internet site at http://www.gale.com

LIBRARY OF CONGRESS CATALOGING-IN-PUBLICATION DATA

Brucken, Kelli M., 1974–
Banshees / by Kelli M. Brucken.
     p. cm. — (Monsters)
Includes index.
ISBN 0-7377-3479-5 (hard cover : alk. paper) 1. Banshees—Ireland. 2. Tales—Ireland.
I. Title. II. Monsters series (KidHaven Press)
GR153.5.B78 2006
398'.45'09417—dc22

                                                                    2005020150

Printed in China

CONTENTS

Chapter 1

A Death Messenger

Ireland has many stories of mythical beings and magical happenings. Legends of ghosts, fairies, and leprechauns have been around for centuries. Among the most famous of these legends are the stories of banshees.

Banshees are female **supernatural** or ghost-like beings who bring warnings of death with their shrill cries. They are heard more often than they are seen. Sometimes banshees wail only minutes before a death occurs. Other times they cry out as many as one or two days before. Either way, legends say that when banshees cry, death is soon to come.

Origins of Banshees

Tales of banshees are highly popular throughout Ireland and Scotland. The banshee first appeared in Irish literature as early as the 8th century. In Gaelic-Irish, a banshee was called the "bean-sidhe," which is pronounced *bann-shee*. The words *bean-sidhe* have been translated to mean "fairy woman," "woman of the otherworld," and "woman of the hills."

A banshee wails, foretelling the death of an unfortunate villager in Ireland.

A boat ride on a moonlit night turns into a terror-filled journey when banshees appear.

Some legends say that banshees are fairies. In these tales banshees are descended from an ancient race of people in Ireland called the Tuatha de Danann. The Danann lived in "hollow hills" or mounds of earth known as sidhe, pronounced *shee*. Eventually the Danann became known as the people of the sidhe, nicknamed "hill folk," "wee folk,"

or "fair folk." As the years passed, fair folk was shortened to fairy.

The name *bean-sidhe* suggests that banshees descended from the Tuatha de Danann. However, banshees are **solitary** beings, while fairies are thought to be very social.

Other legends say that banshees are human spirits. One story says that banshees are the spirits of **keening** women. An old tradition in Ireland measured a person's worth by how many mourners were at his or her funeral. Often times old women were hired by a family to weep at the graveside of a loved one so that their beloved was seen as more popular. These women were known as professional keeners.

Some people believe that banshees are the ghosts of keeners, doomed to cry for the dead as punishment for their insincere grieving when they were alive. Wherever the legends started, they all have one common thread: the banshee's wails.

Who Does a Banshee Visit?

Some tales say that only certain people can hear the cries of a banshee. Others say entire villages are woken by her wails. Some believe that only the person who is fated to die hears the warnings.

This happened in one story that was reported in the magazine *Occult Review* in 1913. The story told of a man named O'Neil and a group of friends who had gathered in Italy. The friends were talking when O'Neil saw a strange-looking woman.

Because he appeared surprised, his friends asked him what was wrong. He told them he had seen a woman with a gleaming face, a mass of red hair, and a horrid expression in her eyes.

One woman in the group said his description sounded like a banshee. O'Neil knew what a banshee was, and he solemnly announced that someone very dear to him would soon be dead. Two hours later he died of a heart attack.

A long-haired banshee rises in the mist on a peaceful lake.

THE SOUND OF A BANSHEE

Those who have heard the howls of banshees and survived are said to never forget the sound. Their cries are described as mournful and lonesome. Rising high in pitch and then low again, their wails can raise the hair on the back of a person's neck and make his or her body break out in a cold sweat.

The sound of a banshee's cries have been compared to animal sounds, such as the screeching of cats or the calls of a bird. One Irishwoman from the county

Cavan describes her experience: "It was a mournful sound. It would put ye in mind of them old yard cats on the wall, but it wasn't cats. I know it myself."[1]

Banshee howls are sometimes so loud they can be heard throughout entire villages. Some say the deaf can even hear their wails. An Irishwoman from the county of Down said: "I heard the banshee; I heard her right here in this town late one night and the ground was shaking under me with the cries of her, she was making the valley echo. Another woman heard her, Ellen Burns and Ellen was deaf, as deaf as a beetle."[2]

Some banshees are described as having great beauty and long red hair.

THE VISIBLE BANSHEE

Although it is more common to hear a banshee than to see one, there are many reports of banshee sightings. The appearance of Irish banshees have been described in a variety of ways. Some people have seen them as beautiful young women with long, flowing blond or reddish hair.

Other people have seen them as hideous old hags with tangled gray hair and a wrinkled face. In certain parts of Ireland they have been seen wearing a green or red dress. Most descriptions tell of a small woman with long white or gray hair. She wears a long plain dress of white or gray and is covered from her neck to her ankles by a cloak. Her eyes are a fiery red from her constant weeping.

The Banshee's Comb

Sometimes a banshee is described as combing her long, flowing hair with a silver comb. The comb is the banshee's most cherished possession. To bother a banshee or her comb is a serious mistake. A banshee has been known to throw her comb at people who interfere with her duties. The result to those unfortunate people is often serious injury—sometimes even death.

If a person should come across a banshee's comb that has been dropped or lost, he or she should leave it alone. There are several tales of people who found a banshee's comb and took it home. One story told in Ireland for many years tells of a man who was out walking late at night. He spotted a woman in a long white gown across a field. As he went to her, he noticed she was combing her hair. He called out, and the woman ran away, dropping her comb as she went. The man picked up the comb and took it home with him. Later that night as he was in bed, a knocking came at his window.

*A look of cruelty shows on the face of a banshee,
who is determined to complete her terrible mission.*

He heard a terrible moaning outside. In horror he realized the comb he had taken must have belonged to a banshee.

He knew he must return the comb to the angry banshee, but he could not return the comb with his bare hand. If a person returns a banshee's comb with a bare hand, the hand may be ripped right from the body. So the man grabbed the comb with iron **tongs** and thrust it out the window. The comb was grabbed with such a force that the tongs were bent and broken when he drew them back in the window.

This man's encounter with a banshee was scary, but he was fortunate. He escaped with his life. Not all who have come in contact with banshees have been so lucky. For no matter what the banshee looks or sounds like, its wail usually means death.

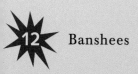

CHAPTER 2

Banshees Around the World

The legend of the banshee has been kept alive for generations through stories in Ireland. Ireland is not the only country that has banshees, however. Supernatural death messengers have also been reported in other countries, such as the United States, Scotland, and Wales.

A TENNESSEE BANSHEE

There are several legends of banshees in the United States. One comes from around the Nolichucky River in Tennessee. In the 1920s, a young man and his wife lived near the Nolichucky River. The man's wife was pregnant with their first child.

One day the man, who was a trapper, was out checking his traps when he heard a horrible howl, like a scream. He thought the sound was coming from a mountain lion. The trapper chased the sound, hoping to catch the animal for its beautiful coat. No matter how far the man traveled, however, the sound never changed. It never got louder and closer, or softer and farther away. The man wandered aimlessly for two hours in search of the giant cat.

Finally he gave up his search and returned home. When he arrived he was shocked to find his wife had gone into labor all by herself. The man tried desperately to help his wife, but there were complications with the birth. He could not help her, and his wife and child both died later that day.

An unlucky soul encounters a banshee in the woods, signaling the death of someone close.

When the man was younger, his grandfather had told him the legend of the banshee. What he experienced that day made him believe in it. He said, "I know now that what I heard in them woods was a banshee. And it was tryin' to tell me to get back home to my wife. But instead, I spent two hours chasin' what I thought was a wildcat. If only I had not been so greedy to get a new pelt and had listened to what the infernal thing was tryin' to tell me."[3]

A full moon lights the way as a mysterious figure—perhaps a banshee—crosses a bridge at night.

THE MARR BANSHEE

Parts of West Virginia and Ohio were settled by many people of Irish and Scottish descent. Along with their customs, the settlers brought their folktales, including legends of banshees.

In 1836 a man named Thomas Marr married a local woman named Mary Disosche. Marr worked as a night watchman on a toll bridge that crossed a

local river. Several times Thomas mentioned to Mary that he had seen a strange robed figure riding a white horse on his way to and from work.

He came across this mysterious figure almost every night, in just about the exact same place. He could not tell if the rider was male or female, because the face was always covered by a hood. If Thomas tried to get close to the horse, it would turn and disappear into the mist.

On one cold morning in 1874, Mary was waiting for Thomas to return from work. As she heard footsteps approaching the house, she hurried to the door. Instead of Thomas, a white horse appeared and stopped in front of the house. A robed figure sat on the horse with its head covered by a veil. It appeared to be a woman.

Disturbed by this sudden appearance, Mary walked outside to find out what the woman wanted. The woman sat in stony silence, but the horse crept closer to Mary. More unnerved then ever, Mary noticed a strange red glow coming from the woman's eyes. Finally the figure spoke: "I am here to tell you, Mary Marr, that Thomas Marr has just died. Say your prayers Lady. I bid you well."[4] With that, the horse and rider wheeled around and disappeared.

Not one hour later, a man who worked with Thomas came to deliver the ghastly news that Thomas was dead. No one knows what really happened to Thomas that night, except that he met his end in the river below the bridge on which he worked.

Scottish Banshee

While Irish banshees have been known to travel to the United States, banshees of other origins are thought to exist as well. In Scotland banshees are thought to be the ghosts of women who died in childbirth. Scottish banshees are called "bean nighe," which means "washerwoman." They have also been called "washerwoman at the ford" and "little washer by the ford."

The bean nighe differs from the Irish banshee in the way she announces death. She can be found at the side of deserted streams and pools washing the blood-soaked clothing of those who are about to die. Legend holds that these banshees are doomed to stay on Earth and do their work until the day their lives would have normally ended, had they not died in childbirth.

A Scottish banshee is quite grotesque. She is said to have only one nostril and one big protruding tooth. She is always dressed in green and has red webbed feet.

A hideously ugly banshee from Scottish lore casts evil wherever she appears.

The bean nighe is generally portrayed as more evil than an Irish banshee is. If one interrupts her washing work she strikes out at their legs with her wet garments. If a person's legs are struck with the garments, the person loses the use of his or her legs. Legend says, though, that if a person sneaks up on a bean nighe and gets between her and the water, he or she will be granted three wishes.

WELSH BANSHEES

The Welsh have legends of banshees as well. One is known as the cyhiraeth, pronounced *ku-HEE-rith*. She is considered an **ancestral spirit**. The cyhiraeth appears in a window of the house where a person is about to die, repeating his or her name over and over. She is described as hideously ugly with tangled and knotted hair, long black teeth, and shriveled arms.

With arms outstretched like wings, a banshee makes her deadly journey along a village street.

The cyhiraeth is also said to pass through a Welsh village by night, groaning and shaking the windows. When she appears to a whole village, it is said that a deadly **epidemic** will strike the townspeople.

Another Welsh banshee is called gwrach y rhibyn, which means "hag of the dribble." She is said to be the spirit of the wife of Avagddu, who, in Welsh mythology, is the lord over death. She has also been called the wife of Teathur, the Irish death god. The hag is also grotesquely ugly. A Welsh man, who claimed to have seen the hag, described her in 1878.

He said she was "a horrible old woman with long red hair and a face like chalk, and great teeth like tusks. . . . She went through the air with a long, black gown trailing along the ground below her arms."[5] She is said to give an unearthly screech and flap batlike wings against the window of one who is to die.

No matter what country they come from, the legend of banshees is kept alive in stories told about them. It will never be known whether there is any truth to these legends. However, those who have experienced them will never forget.

CHAPTER 3

Investigating Banshees

The many legends that swirl around banshees add to their mystery. Do banshees really exist? Some people firmly believe they do, while others are not so sure.

In 1976 the Irish Folklore Department at the University of Dublin sent out a questionnaire about banshees to many Irish residents. The purpose of the questionnaire was to find out what the Irish people believed a banshee was, where the legend began, and how many people believed banshees were real.

The questionnaire contained 24 questions about everything from how a banshee looked, to how she sounded, to what happened to people if they insulted

A banshee screams in the night, casting an eerie gloom over all who hear her wail.

Some people believe the sound of a banshee might actually be the howl of a wolf or the hoot of an owl.

her. Almost 140 questionnaires were filled out and returned. The answers were rich and varied, showing a mixture of belief and disbelief among the citizens of Ireland.

Many people who responded to the questionnaire believed in banshees because of personal experiences they said they had had with one. They thought they had either heard or seen a banshee. These events could have been the result of fear and mourning at a time of death, however. When a family member is dying, the minds of other family members—

Banshees

in their sad state—could easily play tricks on them. They may notice small things, such as a bird crying or a dog or cat yowling, and imagine that the stories they have heard about banshees have come true.

There are stories, however, of people hearing a banshee's cry when they have no idea death is coming. Certainly fear and mourning could not be the cause here. However, when a family member is told about the recent death of another, they may suddenly think about that strange bird or animal sound they heard a day or two before as something different. Possibly they remember the sound as more mournful and shrill than it actually was and connect it to the wail of a banshee.

Banshee or Animal?

Many people who do not believe in banshees are convinced that the cries some people hear are in fact from a bird or other animal. An Irishman from the county of Donegal describes his belief like this:

> Foxes, too, make an eerie noise. . . . It is a wailing noise very much like a human cry. I well remember one night more than ten years ago when I stood by the roadside for perhaps fifteen or twenty minutes studying a fox's wailing. As I approached home a few minutes later, I met a lady in her seventies and she was very frightened indeed. Although I explained to her that it was merely a fox crying I think that she just did not believe me.[6]

Some cries in the night may indeed be the call of a bird or the wail of an animal. To say that all unexplained noises in the night are from birds or animals would be unrealistic, however. People who have lived in the same area for years are most likely accustomed to the sounds of nature around them. They would probably recognize the sounds of familiar birds and animals. This is not always the case, though.

Not all unexplained wails in the night should be considered a banshee either. There could be many perfectly logical explanations for unknown sounds. When a person hears an unfamiliar sound, he or she tends to listen closely and carefully analyze any other sounds, possibly causing small noises to seem much noisier than they actually are.

Seeing Is Believing

Just as some sounds are hard to identify, some sights can also be misleading. A person's eyes can play tricks on him or her. Shadows in the trees might appear to be a banshee to a person who strongly believes they exist.

There have even been stories of people reporting a banshee in the shape of an animal. If a large black crow lands on the windowsill of a dying person's

A banshee seems to emerge from a tree as shadows fall on its branches.

home, a banshee believer might think a banshee has come to call in the form of a crow. One question on the banshee questionnaire asked what animal form some banshees had taken. One person from the county of Fermanagh stated: "Martin Gallagher from Tyrone told me his mother said it was like a butterfly. It cried in the room at the wake. Someone let it out the window. It was a butterfly banshee."[7]

Dressed in a black flowing robe, a person might look like a banshee to an unsuspecting friend.

IMITATING A BANSHEE

Another explanation for banshee sightings could be that someone imitated one. In its survey, the Irish Folklore Department learned of people imitating banshees to cover up crimes such as theft. It seems dressing up as a banshee, or creating sounds like a banshee, could cause a store owner to abandon his or her shop in fright. This would leave the store open to theft.

Another and less serious reason why a person might imitate a banshee is to play a prank. Teenage boys seem most likely to play these practical jokes and their victims are most often women or teenage girls.

Some pranksters even build special equipment to imitate a banshee. A tin can covered in the fur of an animal makes a good banshee imitation. A small hole can be made in the animal hair and the stem of a water plant inserted through the hole. When pulled back and forth through the hole, the stem makes weird sounds. Some people attribute the sound to the call of a banshee.

PASSING ON BELIEFS

The legend of the banshee is an example of folklore passing from generation to generation. Sometimes people believe in banshees simply because family members also believe in them.

Belief in banshees may disappear or lessen with age. Something that may have seemed frightening

Investigating Banshees

29

No one can say for sure whether banshees exist or not.

and possible in childhood may not seem so scary or real in adulthood. Even getting an education may lessen a person's belief in the supernatural. This is especially true when the fields of science tend to provide a reasonable explanation for each occurrence.

Belief in banshees, much like the belief in ghosts or any other supernatural creature, is a personal choice. No one has proven that banshees exist, but neither has anyone proven that they do not exist.

 Banshees

CHAPTER 4

Famous Banshees

The mysterious banshee lives through the tales and legends that are told about her. Her spirit has been brought to life, however, in several movies and books. The legend of the banshee has also crossed over into many forms of popular culture over the years.

MOVIE BANSHEES

There are not many movies that feature banshees. However, there are a few classic and popular movies that introduce banshees to audiences.

One of the most famous banshees appears in the 1959 Walt Disney movie *Darby O'Gill and the Little People*. The movie is set in Ireland. The main character,

Darby O'Gill, is about to lose his job and his home. He plans to search for leprechauns, who he believes can help save his home. While he is out, however, his daughter has an accident in which she falls and hits her head. As O'Gill tries to wake her, he spots a ghostly spirit above her and hears its wail. The banshee has come to announce Katie's doom.

In a wonderful display of special effects, the banshee floats down from the sky. She is covered in a swirling green robe and draws a comb through her long hair. As she gets closer to Darby and Katie, her moans grow louder and louder.

Darby yells at the banshee to go away and throws a lantern at her. The banshee vanishes in a burst of flames, but she is not gone for long. Soon the mournful wails from the sky start again. Darby tries to chase her off with a shovel. The banshee hovers, and with the swipe of one bony finger she calls the **coach-a-bower**, or death coach, to come and take Katie.

The special effects in *Darby O'Gill* were considered to be some of the best of their time. To create the image of a ghostly green banshee descending in the night sky, Disney used two film techniques. One involved shooting two different scenes (the banshee and the night sky) on the same piece of film. The effect was an eerie scene in which the banshee floats down toward Earth. The other technique involved letting in extra light, or overexposing the film, during processing. This gave the

In the Disney film, Darby O'Gill and the Little People, *special effects were used to create lifelike images of leprechauns (pictured) and a ghostly green banshee.*

banshee its green, ghostlike appearance. At the time, many moviegoers and critics agreed that the image of the ghostly green banshee pointing her bony finger and calling for death was indeed a scary sight.

A Harry Potter Banshee

Another movie banshee made her debut in *Harry Potter and the Prisoner of Azkaban*. This movie is based on the popular book by J.K. Rowling.

Harry Potter is a student at the Hogwarts School for Witchcraft and Wizardry. At Hogwarts, students take classes such as herbology (study of herbs), potions (liquid mixtures used to create spells), flying and care of magical creatures.

One of the Hogwarts classes teaches young witches and wizards how to protect themselves from evil. It is called defense against the dark arts. In this class Harry and his classmates are taught how to stop boggarts. Boggarts are creatures that dwell in dark places such as closets and cupboards. When they are released, they turn into whatever the person nearest is most afraid of. They can be stopped by pointing a magic wand and shouting, "Reddikulus!"

When it is Harry's classmate, Seamus Finnigan's, turn to cast his spell, his boggart is a banshee. She appears as a woman with floor-length hair and a bony green-tinged face.

A bony, green-faced banshee was featured in the book Harry Potter and the Prisoner of Azkaban.

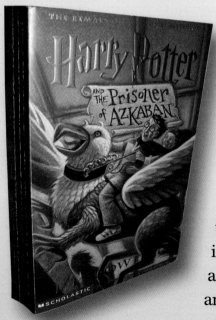

When she opens her mouth, a long wailing shriek emerges that makes Harry's hair stand on end. As Seamus casts his reddikulus spell, the banshee grabs her throat and her shrieks are nothing more than a rasp.

The banshee in *Harry Potter and the Prisoner of Azkaban* was created using computer-generated imagery. This type of special effect uses 3D computer graphics to create an image that would not be possible any other way (since a banshee has never been filmed). It allows a single artist to complete a special effect without the use of actors or oversize props.

A computer-generated image made the banshee in the Harry Potter film look three-dimensional.

BANSHEES IN BOOKS AND COMICS

Hollywood has created some scary banshees, but they can also be found in other places, such as books and comics. The X-men comic books feature a superhero called "Banshee." Banshee is a mutant who has the power to warp reality with the use of his "Sonic Scream." He can fly, shatter solid objects, place people in a temporary trance, and cause people to lose consciousness.

Another place to find banshees is in books. *The Banshee Train* is a spooky tale written by professional storyteller Odds Bodkin. The story is set in Colorado in 1929 and features a train. While traveling through a heavy rainstorm, the engineer and fireman of a train notice a mysterious train behind them. They must speed away before the other train crashes into them. Just before they reach a **trestle**, the first train suddenly stops all by itself. The men hear an eerie scream and see the head of a banshee rising from the train behind them. It is truly frightening, until the men realize the trestle they were about to cross is completely missing. It has been washed out in the rainstorm. Unlike the behavior of banshees in Irish legend, this banshee has saved the lives of all those aboard the train.

BOO!!! Said the Banshee, by Declan Carville, is another ghostly gem of a banshee book. In this story a banshee named Oonagh lives underground with her family. Not a typical banshee, poor Oonagh is afraid of the dark. She feels like a failure because she cannot go out into the night like the rest of her family to do her banshee duties. She is sad until she realizes the wailing of a banshee can happen just as easily in the daytime as it can at night. Her problem is solved.

MUSICAL BANSHEES

The music scene is not without its banshees. In the late 1970s a British punk-rock group named Siouxsie and the Banshees made its debut in London, England.

In the children's book Boo!!! Said the Banshee, *the central character is more terrified than terrifying.*

When the band was trying to decide on a name, *Cry of the Banshee* (a 1970 horror movie) just happened to come on television. The name of the band was born.

Headed by lead singer Siouxsie Sioux, the Banshees were among the longest-lived and most successful punk bands ever. Their career spanned two decades and produced hit records such as "Scream" and "Superstition."

British punk rocker Siouxsie Sioux captured the banshee look in performances with her group, the Banshees.

The name of the punk-rock group Siouxsie and the Banshees *was influenced by the 1970 horror film* Cry of the Banshee.

EDGAR ALLAN POE probes new depths of TERROR!

Vincent PRICE IN

Cry OF THE BANSHEE

Banshees in Sports

Another place to find banshees is in the world of sports. Oakland, California, is home to the professional woman's tackle football team, the Oakland Banshees. They chose the name because the banshee's shriek of death signaled the killing of any other team's hopes of winning a game against them. The team's mission is to give women the opportunity to learn to play tackle football and promote women's athletics. These banshees give their fans a fun and exciting experience at every game.

Whether in legends, movies, books, or the imagination, banshees make a truly impressive image. Though they appear in many ways, one thing is certain—beware of the wail of the banshee!

Notes

Chapter One: A Death Messenger

1. Quoted in Patricia Lysaght, *The Banshee: The Irish Death Messenger.* Boulder, CO: Roberts Reinhart, 1986, p. 73.

2. Quoted in Lysaght, *The Banshee*, p. 76.

Chapter Two: Banshees Around the World

3. Quoted in Linda Linn, "Deadly Wail of the Banshee," Ghost Stories from Kentucky and Tennessee, 2001. http://members.tripod.com/lindaluelinn/index-24.html.

4. Quoted in Susan Sheppard, "Tales of the Banshee," http://magick.wirefire.com/newpage5.htm.

5. Quoted in Richard Holland, "Apparition Has Tidings of Doom," *North Wales Daily Post*, February 23, 2005. http://icnorthwales.icnetwork.co.uk/news/regionalnews.

Chapter Three: Investigating Banshees

6. Quoted in Lysaght, *The Banshee*, p. 226.

7. Quoted in Lysaght, *The Banshee*, p. 111.

GLOSSARY

ancestral spirit: A family spirit; a spirit that is related to the family it haunts.

coach-a-bower: The Irish legend of a death coach that arrives just before someone dies.

epidemic: An outbreak of a disease that spreads quickly and widely.

keening: Wailing or crying loudly for the dead.

solitary: Living or existing alone.

supernatural: Something that is outside of the natural world.

tongs: A tool used for picking things up.

trestle: A supporting tower used underneath a bridge.

FOR FURTHER EXPLORATION

BOOKS

Ita Daly, *Irish Myths and Legends*. Oxford, UK: Oxford University Press, 2001. Ten magical and mystical tales from the land of Ireland. Includes a pronunciation guide and glossary.

Malachy Doyle, *Tales from Old Ireland*. Bath, UK: Barefoot, 2000. Seven classic Irish legends that transport readers to a land far away and long ago. Beautiful soft illustrations bring the magic to life.

Rosalind Kerven, *Looking at Celtic Myths and Legends*. Columbus, OH: NTC, 1998. Enchanting stories filled with the magic of Celtic myth. Includes photographs of Irish artifacts and information-packed sidebars.

Kathleen Krull, *A Pot of Gold: A Treasury of Irish Stories*. New York: Hyperion Children's Books, 2004. Over a dozen exciting Irish tales fill this book along with outstanding full-color illustrations.

James Riordan, *The Kingfisher Treasury of Irish Stories*. New York: Kingfisher, 2004. Seventeen of

Ireland's best tales are brought together in this beautiful book.

WEB SITES

The Banshee from Irelands Eye.com (www.ire landseye.com/animation/explorer/banshee.html). Lots of information on banshees plus other creatures of Irish folklore, such as pookas, changelings, and leprechauns.

A Guide to Irish Culture on the Web (www.irish cultureguide.com/folkmyth.html). A terrific site packed with information on Irish mythology and folklore.

Irish Creatures (http://wolfdragon.net/animals/ irish_creatures/index.php). Wonderful descriptions of some of Ireland's most intriguing creatures, including the banshee.

INDEX

Picture Credits

ABOUT THE AUTHOR

Kelli M. Brucken is the author of many works of nonfiction for children. Her other book for Kid-Haven Press is *Bristlecone Pines*. She makes her home in Auburn, Kansas, where she lives with her husband and two children.